The **Ten** *Marys*
and the Angel Gabriel

The *Ten* Marys
and the Angel Gabriel

Aurora Magni

ILLUSTRATIONS BY
Francesca Vignaga

Paulist Press
New York / Mahwah, NJ

Translation by Rev. Wayne L. Ball

English translation copyright © 2011 by Paulist Press, Inc.

Originally published as *Le dieci Marie...e l'angelo bambino* by PAOLINE Editoriale Libri
©2009 FIGLIE DI SAN PAOLO
Via Francesco Albani, 21 – 20149 Milano--Italy

ISBN: 978-0-8091-6764-7

Published by Paulist Press
997 Macarthur Boulevard
Mahwah, New Jersey 07430

www.paulistpress.com

Printed and bound in Stevens Point, Wisconsin (USA)
by Worzalla
November 2011

Mary the daughter of
James

Mary the daughter of
John

Mary the daughter of
Barnabas

Mary the daughter of
Juda

Mary the daughter of
Mark

Mary the daughter of
Matthew

Mary the daughter of
Simon

Mary the daughter of
Andrew

Mary the daughter of
Joseph

Mary of the laundry

Little angel Gabriel wandered through the desert of Palestine. He was filled with pride. God had surprised him with a very important job. He—little Gabriel himself!—was to announce to a young girl that she would become the mother of God.

All she had to do was say yes.

"This will be easy," he thought, smiling. "Any girl would accept such a great honor."

There was just one tiny problem. He didn't know how to find her.

He should have followed the advice of the older angels:

"Dress up, and be on your best behavior!" one had said.

And another: "You're bringing her good news, so smile!"

The most important advice had come from the Archangel Michael himself:

"Go *straight* to her house. Just appear out of nowhere, the way only angels can. Tell her the good news. She'll be so happy that she'll say yes immediately, and you'll be back here in no time." The Archangel finished up by adding, "God is trusting you with a really *big* mission."

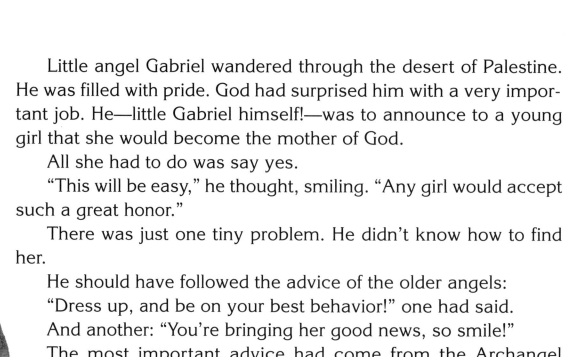

But Gabriel wanted to go sightseeing first.

That was why he didn't look like an angel. No shining white clothes. No bright lights. He couldn't sightsee that way. Besides, an angel might scare the young girl. He would present himself politely as a regular boy instead. He would use his wings and halo only at the end if they were necessary.

But he still had his one tiny problem. He still didn't know how to find her.

He knew the girl lived in Nazareth. He knew her name was Mary. He'd even been given a map of the town with her house circled in red. But he'd forgotten to take the map, and now he didn't have time to go back to heaven and get it.

The older angels had been puzzled that God had chosen such a *little* messenger for such a *big* message. "Maybe they were right," Gabriel thought. "Maybe I *am* too little."

But he liked to be positive! How hard could it be to find a young girl named Mary in a small town like Nazareth? He didn't know who she was. He didn't know where she lived. But when he saw her, he'd recognize her immediately. He was sure of it.

In the distance he spotted Nazareth, its white houses shining in the warm morning sun.

"It's after eight. This young Mary will already be awake and at work," he thought.

He hurried into town toward the market square, following the voices of the buyers and sellers and the sounds of their animals. People had traveled from the countryside to show their wares: carpets, baskets, jugs. One woman was buying fish, and another was just arriving, leading her son.

The little angel looked around. In the distance, at the village laundry basin, a young girl was busy washing clothes, singing to herself as she worked. Nearby was a tall gangly man, chewing on a small stick and holding a donkey tied on a rope.

Gabriel stepped up to the man.

"Good morning, sir! Are you from this town?"

"Yes, I live nearby. Who are you, and where are you from?" asked the man, looking down at him.

"I've come from far away to find someone. It's very important for me to find her."

"Ah, a relative! I know everybody. Who are you looking for?"

"I know she lives in Nazareth. I know her name is Mary. It shouldn't be hard to find her, right? The town is so small."

The man laughed. "My boy, where have you lived until now? Mary is a very common name. In fact, most of the women in Nazareth are called Mary! Is your Mary tall or short? Young or old? Pretty or ugly? Rich or poor? We have *every* kind of Mary here. My master's daughter is named Mary. Even the girl washing laundry is named Mary! Do you know the name of her husband?"

"Um...no...."

"Well, then, the name of her father?"

"No...not that either."

"Well, if you're looking for a relative, of *course* you at least know what she looks like, more or less. Don't you?"

Gabriel was becoming nervous. He didn't know any of this! He tried to imagine what the mother of God would look like.

"She's beautiful," he answered at last. "Yes, she's probably *very* beautiful. She's young, and she's not married. That's all I know."

The man scratched his head and thought for a good long while. Then he took the small stick out of his mouth, stuck it in his pocket, and said:

"Okay. You're looking for a young girl, right? So we'll leave out all the old women. And this young girl isn't married, right? So we'll leave out all the married women. That leaves about ten Marys: Mary the daughter of John, Mary the daughter of Barnabas, Mary the daughter of Juda, Mary the daughter of Mark, Mary the daughter of Matthew, Mary the daughter of Simon, Mary the daughter of Andrew, Mary the daughter of Joseph, and, of course, Mary the daughter of James, my master," he concluded.

"That's not too many," said the little angel. "Tell me about your master's daughter. My Mary will certainly be from a good family."

"Well, this one's the best! Mary of James is noble and rich. She lives in the great palace over there at the edge of the square. If I didn't have to sell this donkey, I'd go with you."

"Don't worry, sir. And if she's the girl I'm looking for, I'll tell your master you were a big help," the angel said, with his heart lightened. His mission was almost at an end! "So long, Bartholomew!"

The man stared in confusion.

"How did he know my name?" he wondered, scratching his head. He shrugged, searched in his pocket for the small stick, and stuck it back in his mouth.

Gabriel raised his eyes toward the great palace and exclaimed, "Surely, the future mother of my Lord lives here! The Son of God will obviously be born in a huge house like this and grow up to be a powerful man."

Before he could knock, the door opened as if by magic. He crossed through the palace, admiring the rooms. No one noticed him at all. At last, he stepped out into a luxurious garden in which a beautiful young maiden was walking.

"Hail, Mary," he said to her in a sweet tone.

As soon as she saw him, she became angry.

"Beggars aren't allowed in my house. Go back to your pigsty!" She screamed for her servants: "Come quickly! A beggar broke in! Hurry! Throw him out before he robs me!"

Gabriel managed to get far away. Surely, this was not the Mary he was looking for. The Mother of God couldn't possibly have such a hard heart.

He walked back to the square to search for the *right* Mary.

Once more he found his friend Bartholomew.

"Well, young man, how did it go? Was that the right Mary?"

"No," answered the angel. "She was noble and rich, but she was very unkind. Who should I try next?"

"Let me think. Mary of John lives nearby. She's the daughter of one of the richest merchants in the village. She lives in that big house just past the square. She's hard-working. At this hour you should find her at her weaving."

The angel said good-bye and went off.

When he arrived, once more the door opened all by itself without making a sound. He silently crossed through the house and then came upon a workroom. There, a young girl was busy telling a group of weavers what to do.

"No time to lose! Everything has to be ready by tonight! Let me count how many pieces are already finished and folded."

She hurried toward the storeroom. The angel stepped in front of her and said:

"Hail, Mary."

"What are you doing here?" she asked sternly. "In this house we don't tolerate laziness. Get back to work or I'll fire you!"

"But I'm here to bring you good news."

The girl looked at him, put her hands on her hips, and snapped, "The only good news you can give me is that you're leaving! I don't have time to waste listening to little boys like you. Get out before I throw you out!"

Without a word, Gabriel left. That was definitely *not* the Mary he was looking for. The mother of God couldn't possibly be too busy for other people.

Going back to the square, he found Bartholomew again.

"My friend, I can see from your face that this time did not go well either," the man said. "Don't be discouraged. Try Mary of Barnabas. She's the most beautiful girl in the village. Her parents adore her, and every young man in town has proposed to her."

"Where does she live?" asked Gabriel.

"The house is right around the corner. You'll recognize it immediately. There are always two or three young men hanging around, hoping she'll appear at the window."

Gabriel hurried round the corner, slipped past all the young men, and entered the house without making a sound. He came to a room in which a beautiful young maiden was gazing at herself in the mirror. "Surely *she* must be the future mother of my Lord!" Gabriel said. "The Son of God will obviously have the most *beautiful* mother in the world!"

He stepped a bit closer. "Hail, Mary," he said to her.

"Hail, handsome young man," the maiden graciously responded.

"I am here to bring you good news," Gabriel said, as his spirits lifted.

"Good news? Have more gifts arrived for me? I would love a beautiful embroidered gown. Yesterday the baker's daughter had on a red dress. It was exquisite—but it would look so much better on *me*. My parents have no money left to buy a dress like it, but they're working overtime, and by the end of the month they'll…"

The angel said a quick good-bye and left, while the girl still sat staring at herself in the mirror. The Mother of God couldn't possibly be vain.

Returning once more to the square, he found Bartholomew, who tried to console him.

"My poor boy, still no luck! Try Mary of Juda, the daughter of the carpenter. Her family isn't rich, but they are good people. You can't go wrong with this one. The house is the last one on the street down there at the end," he added, pointing.

After a bit of a walk, the angel arrived at the house of Juda. Unseen, he passed through the workshop—right under the carpenter's nose! In the kitchen, he found a girl kneading dough to make bread.

"Hail, Mary," the angel greeted her.

Terrified, she jumped back.

"Who are you? What do you want?" she asked. "You're not going to hurt me, I hope."

"Certainly not," Gabriel reassured her. "I have come to bring you good news."

"Good news? It could be *bad* news. I don't want to know anything about anything. You frighten me. Mama, help! I'm scared! But she'll just think I'm getting upset over nothing again! Papa, come quickly! There's a stranger here who means to hurt me!"

The angel left while the girl was still crying out in fear.

"That's not the Mary I'm looking for. The mother of God cannot be so timid," he murmured. Shaking his head, he returned to the square.

Next Bartholomew
suggested *Mary of Mark*. "Her
father comes from Greece," he said,
"but her mother is Jewish and she is, too.
Perhaps *this* Mary is the right one."

The angel drew near to the house. In the
courtyard garden, he saw a beautiful girl wearing
a white dress designed in a Greek style.

"Hail, Mary," said the angel.

The girl was surprised but not startled.

"Greetings to you, O foreigner."

"I bring you good news. I speak to you in the name of our God."

"Which God?" she asked.

"The God of Abraham, Isaac, and Jacob," Gabriel responded quickly.

"I don't know what good news *your* God can have for me. Zeus is much more powerful, as well as Poseidon, Athena, and the other gods. This is what my father taught me."

Disheartened, the angel left.

"Surely, the Son of God would not be born to a girl who did not even believe in God," he whispered to himself as he returned to the square.

He found his friend again and said, "Dear Bartholomew, not even that one was the right Mary. What am I going to do?"

"Unfortunately there aren't many left. Try the house of Matthew the potter. He lives on the outskirts of town, in a house covered in frescos. His only daughter is always home."

The angel thanked him and began to walk. He soon found the house and slipped inside.

"The house is truly elegant. And the rooms are neat and clean," he observed with an air of approval.

In the kitchen, a woman was busy working while a girl sat in a chair with her hands in her lap.

"Mary, can you fetch me some water from the well?"

"In this heat, Mother? I'll faint."

The mother sighed.

"Then, could you knead the bread for me?" she asked.

"I don't want to. I'm too tired."

"Daughter, you can't sit around all day doing nothing. If you don't learn how to take care of a house now, what will you do when you're married?"

"I'm going to marry a rich man, with lots of servants. I don't like to work."

"Can you at least pass me the flour?" asked the mother.

"I don't even know where it is. I'm going out to the garden to get some air."

Gabriel didn't bother to talk to her.

"A girl this lazy cannot possibly be the mother of my Lord," he said to himself, as once more he returned to the square.

"My friend Bartholomew, who's left?" the angel asked, with just a thread of a voice.

The man scratched his head.

"My dear boy, are you sure the girl still lives in Nazareth? Just last year, three families moved to Jerusalem and among them were at least two Marys."

"The girl lives here. I'm sure of it. Help me one more time, please."

"There aren't many Marys left. The daughter of Simon the cart driver. The daughter of Andrew the carpenter. Oh—and the daughter of Joseph the goat-herder."

"Who's Joseph the goat-herder?" asked the angel, curious.

"He's an old man who raises goats. But he loves all animals. He has a great gift for healing and can cure them as well. Everyone goes to Joseph when an animal is sick."

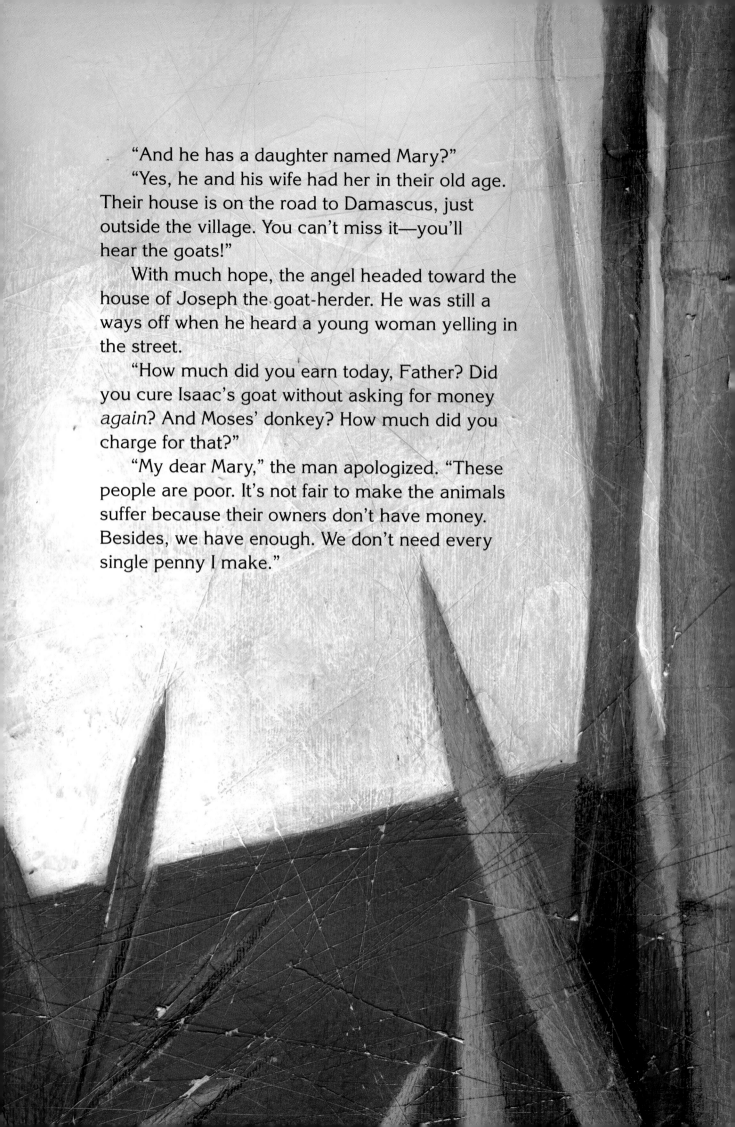

"And he has a daughter named Mary?"

"Yes, he and his wife had her in their old age. Their house is on the road to Damascus, just outside the village. You can't miss it—you'll hear the goats!"

With much hope, the angel headed toward the house of Joseph the goat-herder. He was still a ways off when he heard a young woman yelling in the street.

"How much did you earn today, Father? Did you cure Isaac's goat without asking for money *again*? And Moses' donkey? How much did you charge for that?"

"My dear Mary," the man apologized. "These people are poor. It's not fair to make the animals suffer because their owners don't have money. Besides, we have enough. We don't need every single penny I make."

"I don't care, Father. Go back and demand what they owe you!"

Hearing this, the angel turned around and retraced his steps.

"This young girl is greedy. She cannot be the one I am looking for."

By now, sun was high in the sky and it was becoming quite hot. Bartholomew was sitting under the only tree at the edge of the square, trying to cool off. He saw Gabriel and made a place for him under the branches close to the tree's trunk.

"My friend, there are only two possibilities left. Mary of Simon and Mary of Andrew. They live next door to each other, ten minutes from here. I'll tell you the way."

Gabriel set off again.

All of a sudden he heard two girls arguing in the street.

"Mary of Simon!" shouted one girl. "Stay away from my boyfriend Barnabas!"

"*Your* boyfriend?" the other yelled back. "Mary of Andrew, you're a thief! You stole *my* boyfriend. I hate you!"

"I hate you too!"

Gabriel stopped dead in his tracks. Neither of these two Marys could be the one he was looking for. A girl with so much hatred in her heart could not possibly be the mother of the Son of God.

Completely exhausted, the angel walked back to the square.

The market was empty. Even Bartholomew and his donkey had left. Only the girl at the laundry basin remained, but she was gathering up her things to go home, too.

The scorching sun had made the little angel incredibly thirsty. He walked over to the basin.

"Hail, Maiden. I'm very thirsty. Do you have a bowl?"

The girl took her small wooden bowl, filled it with water, and gave it to him.

"You're a stranger here," she said with great kindness. She had big dark eyes and a sweet smile that warmed Gabriel's heart. "I see that you are tired," she continued. "Please come back to my house and rest and have a bowl of soup. My father and mother will gladly welcome you."

"I can't," he said. "I'm searching for a girl, but I don't know where she lives. I've searched the entire village and still have not found her."

"If you tell me who she is, perhaps I can help you."

"Her name is Mary."

The girl shook her head. "Your search won't be easy because that's such a common name. Even *my* name is Mary." Once more her face lit up with the sweetest smile.

Gabriel's heart suddenly told him that *this* girl was the Mary he had been searching for!

His face became radiant as only that of an angel can be.

"Greetings, favored one!" he said. "The Lord is with you."

But the young girl was much perplexed by his words and pondered what sort of greeting this might be.

The angel said to her, "Do not be afraid, Mary, for you have found favor with God. And now, you will conceive in your womb and bear a son, and you will name him Jesus. He will be great and will be called the Son of the Most High, and the Lord God will give to him the throne of his ancestor David. He will reign over the house of Jacob forever, and of his kingdom there will be no end."

Mary said to the angel, "How can this be, since I am a virgin?"

The angel said to her, "The Holy Spirit will come upon you, and the power of the Most High will overshadow you; therefore, the child to be born will be holy; he will be called Son of God. And now, your relative Elizabeth in her old age has also conceived a son; and this is the sixth month for her who was said to be barren. For nothing will be impossible with God."

Then Mary said, "Here am I, the servant of the Lord; let it be with me according to your word."

Then the angel departed from her.

(Luke 1:28–38)

ABOUT THE AUTHOR:

Aurora Magni is an electrical engineer by profession who writes stories and fables in her spare time. In a small way, *The Ten Marys* sums up the sense of joyful expectation in the Gospel accounts of the birth of Jesus.

ABOUT THE ILLUSTRATOR:

Francesca Vignaga is an award-winning illustrator who lives and works in Vicenza, Italy. Her first love is illustrating books for children.